This story is retold from "The Field of Boliauns,"
included by folklorist T. Crofton Croker
in *Legends and Traditions of the South of Ireland* (1825).

ISBN 0-590-43170-6

All rights reserved. Published by Scholastic Inc.,
730 Broadway, New York, NY 10003, by arrangement with
Lothrop, Lee & Shepard Books, a division of William Morrow & Company.

20 19 18 17 16 15 14 13   9/9 0 1 2/0

Printed in the U.S.A.   08
First Scholastic printing, February 1990

Clever Tom and the Leprechaun

Retold and Illustrated by Linda Shute

SCHOLASTIC INC.

New York Toronto London Auckland Sydney

To Libby Thomson, with love.

Clever Tom
and the
Leprechaun

One fine day,
on Lady-day in the harvest,
Tom Fitzpatrick took a ramble
down the lane.
Click-clack, click-clack,
he heard through the hedge.
So Tom tiptoed closer
to take a look.

The clacking sound stopped
when Tom peeped through the bushes,
and in the shadow, what did he see?

Why, a big gallon pitcher
and a teeny tiny man
with a brown leather apron
and a three-cornered hat.

Up the small man climbed
on his wee wooden stool
and dipped his little piggin
into the crock. Then
he settled down, with his
full mug beside him,
to hammer on the heel of a
fairy-sized shoe.

"By the powers!" thought
Tom. "It's a leprechaun!
If I catch him and scare him,
he'll give me his gold.
Since I'm a clever fellow,
that should be simple.
Before the sun sets,
I'll have my fortune made!"

Tom stared at the leprechaun and tried not to blink. He knew that if he looked away, the old man would escape. Then he crept up quite near and tipped his hat politely, saying, "Good day to you, neighbor. Blessings on your work."

"Thank you kindly," said the small one, but he never looked up. He just kept on tapping at the heelpiece of the brogue.

Tom moved his hand closer
while he smiled very sweetly
and said, "Today's a holiday.
You shouldn't have to work."
    The leprechaun frowned
and answered Tom sharply,
"If I do, that's my business
and none of your own! Instead
of pestering me, young man,
you ought to be watching your
father's fields. Look there!
The cows have broke into the oats!
See? They're knocking the corn
all about!"
    Cows in the cornfield?
Tom's head started turning…

But he wasn't fooled by the leprechaun's trick.
Quickly he grabbed the sly fellow and cried,
"Now you're my prisoner! Tell me, where is your gold?"
   The leprechaun wiggled and twisted and whined,
"I'm just a poor man," but Tom held him fast.
   "You and I both know you're lying," said Tom,
and he made a fierce, frightening face.

Finally, the leprechaun quit squirming and said, "Tom Fitzpatrick, you're too clever for me. I see you are after my buried treasure, so I'll have to show you where it is hid."

With his eye on the bitty man
locked in his fist, Tom followed
where the leprechaun led him.
He traipsed over a hill
and under some hedges

and through a ditch
and across the peat bog.
At last, just when Tom
feared he'd been hoodwinked,

he found himself in a great field of weeds.

"Dig there," said the leprechaun, pointing to a bush. "Deep under that boliaun is where I put my gold."

"Thunderation!" said Tom. "I need to fetch my spade, but when I return I'll be lost. There are forty acres of boliauns here, and each plant looks just like the other."

Still watching the leprechaun, Tom figured out a plan. He tied his bright red garter on the bush. "Swear, you old rascal, that you won't take this off while I run back to get my spade."

"That I will promise you," the little man said. (Tom grinned, knowing leprechauns always keep their word.) "Now, since I have shown you where my treasure is, I don't suppose you'll need me anymore."

"No," said Tom. "My fortune's made. You may go, and good luck go with you."

"Then good-bye, Tom Fitzpatrick," said the leprechaun. "May you do much good with what you find."

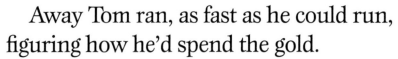

Away Tom ran, as fast as he could run,
figuring how he'd spend the gold.

Then back he came, with his shovel in his hand,
back to the field of boliauns.

But when he got there, lo and behold! a garter, just like his own, was tied to each and every bush as far as he could see.

Tom dug under the boliaun
where he thought he'd tied his garter.
But nothing was buried under that bush,
and so he dug under another.

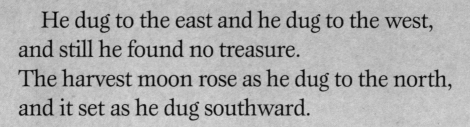

He dug to the east and he dug to the west,
and still he found no treasure.
The harvest moon rose as he dug to the north,
and it set as he dug southward.

When the sun came up, Tom saw he'd dug a hundred holes.
And tired Tom Fitzpatrick knew he couldn't find that gold,
so he gave up and headed for home.

From then on, Tom always carried his spade, and he never stopped listening for a tapping in the field. Every chance he got, he'd tell how he nearly found the gold. "And since I'm a clever fellow," Tom would end his tale, "the *next* time I catch that leprechaun, I'll have my fortune made!"

SOURCE NOTES

When he was a teenager, T. Crofton Croker (1798–1854) rambled in the countryside near his native Cork and listened to the Irish peasants' stories, ballads, and keens. Croker's *Legends and Traditions of the South of Ireland*, the first published collection of Irish folklore, included the archetypical leprechaun tale "The Field of Boliauns."

The story is thought to have its origins in Celtic lands. Although Croker learned it in English, not Gaelic, it was found only among Irish Celts, decendants of the people that migrated from Europe to the British Isles around 400 B.C. and formed the dominant culture there for over a thousand years. Today Britain's Celtic population is found in Ireland, the Scottish Highlands, Wales, and the Isle of Man.

The tale's motif of marking many things identically to prevent one of them from being discovered is found worldwide. The leprechaun, however, is exclusively Irish. No elves, trolls, or other fairy folk appear in ancient Celtic legends and sagas, but these beings are found in the lore of the countries to the north. This has led to the speculation that the Irish leprechaun may be a legacy of the "Danish" (Viking or Norse) conquest of A.D. 795–1014.

Boliaun (pronounced bowl-YAWN) is derived from *buachall'an,* the Gaelic name for the plant known as ragwort, sometimes called ragweed because of the ragged shape of the leaf. Ragwort has long been associated with fairy folk. Like rye grass, it is their refuge and cannot be used against them. Fairies are said to magically change the stalks of the ragwort to horses which they ride through the air. The Greek goddess Hecate and other witches flew ragwort sticks when no broomstick was handy. In Ireland ragwort grows to be a large noxious weed, which farmers destroy because it is harmful to animals that graze on it.

Lady-days are celebrations of events in the life of Our Lady, the Virgin Mary: the feast of the Annunciation on March 25, which in medieval times was the first legal day of the new year; the Assumption on August 15; the Birth on September 8; and the Immaculate Conception on December 8. In Ireland, there were many local festivals on March 25 and August 15. People tried to start reaping their grain crops around the time of the August holiday. Today sheep and horses are still brought to village fairs at that time, and the faithful visit holy wells popularly dedicated to Our Lady, circling the wells as they say their prayers.

Irish shrubs and wildflowers are shown here as they would look on this "Lady-day in the harvest." Nowadays in Britain March 25 is designated Lady Day.

The buried gold the leprechauns are said to hoard is part of the treasure left behind by "the Danes," meaning the Vikings. These invaders raided and pillaged Ireland from A.D. 795 until 1014, when Brian Boroimhe, High King of Ireland, defeated them at the battle of Clontarf near Dublin. Beautiful artifacts of beaten gold have in fact been dug from the Irish bogs, including a marvelously crafted scale-model Viking warship.

In Scotland and Ireland, people believed that the Danes had a recipe for making beer from heather. Legend has it that King Boroimhe once imprisoned several Danish brewmasters, hoping to learn their formula. The eldest, fearing his comrades would tell, promised the king he'd reveal it after Boroihme killed the others. Then he carried the secret to his death. After the Danes were gone, only leprechauns were thought to know and guard the secret. In "The Field of Boliauns," Tom begs for a taste of what the leprechaun claims is ale made of heather.

Leprechauns, as they are now called, are Solitary fairies. They are usually discovered by the tapping sounds they make mending tiny slippers as they sit in some lonely spot behind a wall, in a hedge, under tree roots, or in a ruined castle. Industrious and irascible, they keep apart from the sociable Trooping fairies, who live in splendor and on moonlit nights sing sweetly and dance holes into those slippers.

When this story was first recorded, the fairies' shoemaker was called by various names throughout Ireland: *logheryman* in Ulster, *luricaune* in Kerry, *lurigadaune* in Tipperary, *lurikeen* in Kildare, *leprechaune* in Leinster, and *cluricaune* in Cork. Croker regarded these as regional variants of *luacharma'n,* the Irish word for pygmy. He called the wee man a cluricaune.

However, some say that a cluricaune is a different creature, a gloomy, grouchy fellow who hangs about in cellars drinking ale and smoking a dudeen (clay pipe). Others claim a cluricaune is simply a leprechaun on a spree.

In contrast to the Trooping fairies, who are known for wearing green, the leprechaun is recognized by his red jacket, in Kerry a cutaway with two rows of seven brass buttons. Some people say his breeches are yellow, others say scarlet, and on the cold damp west coast they say he wears a drab frieze overcoat. But he is always seen in a leather apron and high-heeled shoes with ostentatiously large silver buckles.

The leprechaun is said to have descended from an evil spirit and a renegade fairy, which accounts for his mixed nature: merry and generous one minute, moody and mischievous the next. As a trickster, he can't be outsmarted. Typically, he escapes his captors by blowing dust or snuff into their eyes to make them blink, or by distracting them so they look away. No one has ever managed to cheat him out of his gold.